A FISH FOR MRS. GARDENIA

BY YOSSI ABOLAFIA

Greenwillow Books

New York

Watercolors and a black pencil were used for the
full-color art. The text type is ITC Usherwood.

Printed in Hong Kong by South China Printing Co.
First Edition   1 2 3 4 5 6 7 8 9 10

Library of Congress Cataloging-in-Publication Data

Abolafia, Yossi.
A fish for Mrs. Gardenia / by Yossi Abolafia.   p.   cm.
Summary: A series of haphazard events threatens to spoil Mr. Bennett's
dinner with Mrs. Gardenia after his fish disappears from his outside
grill, but a final accident returns the fish to its rightful place.
ISBN 0-688-07467-7. ISBN 0-688-07468-5 (lib. bdg.)
[1. Humorous stories.]   I. Title.   II. Title: A Fish for Mrs. Gardenia.
PZ7.A165Fi 1988   [E]—dc19   87-17907   CIP   AC

For the Sidon family

Whenever Mrs. Gardenia sat in the park, reading or feeding the birds, Mr. Bennett would stand nearby, pretending to fish. He was very much in love with Mrs. Gardenia, but too shy to tell her.

Mrs. Gardenia was fond of Mr. Bennett, but since her husband had died she kept mostly to herself, hardly talking to anyone.

One Friday afternoon, Mr. Bennett actually caught a big fish! Astonished and proud, he showed it to Mrs. Gardenia.

"That would make a lovely supper," she said, which gave Mr. Bennett the courage to say,

"Would you care to join me for dinner tonight, Mrs. Gardenia?"
"Well," she said, "that's very kind of you, but…"
She paused for a minute and then said,
"Yes, I'd like to come."

Back at home, Mr. Bennett marinated the fish in lemon juice, garlic, and olive oil.
Then he went outside to light the barbecue.

Next door, nosy Mrs. Murgle poked her head out the window to see what Mr. Bennett was cooking. He was in such good spirits that he decided to show Mrs. Murgle the fish and save her the trouble of guessing.

When he took the fish out of the bowl, it was so slippery that it shot from his fingers and flew right into Mrs. Murgle's window.

Mrs. Murgle screamed.
She grabbed the fish and
threw it as far as she could.

The milkman down the street didn't hear the splash in his milk can.

When he poured milk for Mrs. Prunish, she said,
"Funny, I smell fish…"

When he poured milk for Mrs. Slokum, she dropped her pitcher.

"A fish in the milk! Yech!!" she shouted.

"I don't understand how it got there," said the milkman.

Mrs. Slokum slammed the door.

The milkman picked up the fish and drove away.
"If I can't sell my milk," he thought, "I might be
able to sell the fish."

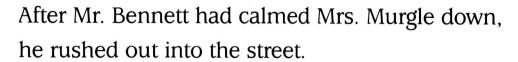

After Mr. Bennett had calmed Mrs. Murgle down,
he rushed out into the street.
"Did you see a fish fly by?" he asked Mrs. Slokum.
"The milkman might know something," she
mumbled. "I don't know anything anymore."

At the corner of McDonald and Pine, Mr. Bennett caught up with the milkman.

"I sold the fish to a man in a polka-dot suit," said the milkman.

"Which way did he go?" asked Mr. Bennett.

"I didn't notice," said the milkman.

Mr. Bennett walked sadly down the street.
"What will I do now? What will I serve
  Mrs. Gardenia for dinner?" he muttered.
"How about a chicken?" asked the butcher.
"But I promised her a fish," said Mr. Bennett.
  Nevertheless, he bought a chicken.

When he got home, Mr. Bennett prepared
the chicken and placed it on the hot grill.
Then he went inside to make a salad.

Normie Cooper stopped and stared at the sizzling chicken. "A piece of chicken before dinner won't spoil my appetite," he thought.

Next door, Mrs. Murgle sniffed once, then twice.
"It's barbecued chicken," she said, and rushed
to the window.

Frightened by Mrs. Murgle's sudden appearance, Normie grabbed the whole chicken and hid behind the fence. Mrs. Murgle stared at the empty grill. Puzzled, she left the window to greet her husband, who had just walked in—

wearing his polka–dot suit.

"Guess what I brought us for supper, dear!"

he said with a smile.

"A fish!" she yelled. "I almost had one right in my face today! Get rid of that fish and bring me a chicken!" Mr. Murgle put the fish back in his basket and left to get her a chicken.

Normie had just crept out of Mr. Bennett's yard when he saw Mrs. Gardenia walking to the front door.

He turned quickly and ran right into Mr. Murgle. The fish sailed out of the basket and landed on Mr. Bennett's hot grill. Normie dropped the chicken and ran home.

When Mrs. Gardenia saw Mr. Murgle lying in the street, she helped him up, picked up the chicken, and put it in his basket.

Mr. Murgle limped back home.

"That's exactly what I wanted!" said his wife,

when she saw the chicken.

At seven o'clock sharp, Mrs. Gardenia rang
Mr. Bennett's doorbell.
"The fish smells delicious," she said.
"It's a chicken," said Mr. Bennett apologetically.

"I may be old," said Mrs. Gardenia, "but I can still tell a chicken from a fish."

Mr. Bennett's mouth dropped open.

Mr. Bennett and Mrs. Gardenia had many lovely
dinners together in the years that followed.
Whenever they had chicken, it reminded him of fish.

But whenever they had fish, he made sure to cook it indoors.